The Berenstain Bears.

THE TROUBLE
WITH TRYOUTS

The Berenstain Bears®
THE TROUBLE WITH TRYOUTS

Stan, Jan, and Mike Berenstain

ZONDER**kidz**™

ZONDERKIDZ

The Berenstain Bears The Trouble with Tryouts
Copyright © 2019 by Berenstain Publishing, LLC
Illustrations © 2019 by Berenstain Publishing, LLC

Portions of this books were previously published with the title *The Berenstain Bears Too Small for the Team* copyright © 2003 by Berenstain Enterprises, Inc.

Requests for information should be addressed to:
Zonderkidz, 3900 Sparks Dr. SE, Grand Rapids, Michigan 49546

Library of Congress Cataloging-in-Publication Data

Names: Berenstain, Stan, 1923-2005, author. | Berenstain, Jan, 1923-2012, author. |
    Berenstain, Mike, 1951- author.
Title: The Berenstain Bears the trouble with tryouts : an early reader chapter book / Stan
    and Jan Berenstain and Mike Berenstain.
Other titles: Too small for the team
Description: Grand Rapids, MI : Zonderkidz, [2019] | Summary: Although she is a very
    good soccer player, Sister Bear is not allowed to try out for the team until she is
    bigger, and so she signs up to be the team manager in hopes of proving herself to
    the coach. |
Identifiers: LCCN 2019010279 (print) | LCCN 2019012909 (ebook) |,ISBN 9780310767879
    (ebook) | ISBN 9780310767893 (audio download) | ISBN 9780310767831 (paperback)
    | ISBN 9780310767886 (hardcover)
Subjects: | CYAC: Soccer—Fiction. | Size—Fiction. | Sportsmanship—Fiction. |
    Bears—Fiction.
Classification: LCC PZ7.B4483 (ebook) | LCC PZ7.B4483 Bfgc 2019 (print) | DDC
    [Fic]—dc23
LC record available at https://lccn.loc.gov/2019010279

Art direction: Cindy Davis
Interior design: Denise Froehlich

Printed in the United States of America

19 20 21 22 23 / LSC / 10 9 8 7 6 5 4 3 2 1

1

One fine spring day Sister was in gym class. The class was playing soccer.

Sister loved soccer. She was fast. She could run like the wind.

She was tricky too. She could change direction in a flash. She could twist and twirl.

And she could kick. Boy, could she kick! She could kick a soccer ball from midfield all the way to the goal.

Sister had a great game during gym class. She stole the ball seven times. She made an out-of-bounds kick that went way down the field.

She even scored *three* goals.

There was one problem. Coach Brown wasn't watching very closely. She was on the phone during gym class and missed most of the game. She was the gym teacher *and* the girls' soccer coach. And she didn't see any of Sister's goals.

At the end of class, Coach Brown came back to the field. She told the class to line up.

"I have an announcement to make," she said. "Tryouts for the girls' soccer team are next Wednesday, after school. The tryouts are for older, bigger girls. But a few of you might be big enough to play. I'll give you a chance. Okay, time to hit the showers."

In the shower, Sister said to her best friend Lizzy Bruin, "Isn't it great about soccer tryouts?"

Lizzy shrugged. "For the girls who get to try out, it is."

"Aren't you going to?" asked Sister. "You're good."

"Didn't you hear Coach Brown?" said Lizzy. "The soccer team is for bigger, older girls. I bet Coach Brown wouldn't even let me try out."

"Well, I'm going to try out," said Sister.

Lizzy gave Sister a funny look. "But you're no bigger than I am," she said. "Coach Brown won't let you try out, either."

"Then why did she invite us?" asked Sister.

Lizzy pointed at Laura Goodbear. "Because of cubs like her."

"She's our age," said Sister.

"Sure," said Lizzy. "But she's *twice* as big."

It was true. Laura was way taller than Sister and Lizzy. She looked two or three years older.

"So what?" said Sister. "I'm a better player than Laura."

"Coach Brown didn't get to see you play," said Lizzy. "She was on the phone."

Sister frowned. Then she stopped frowning.

"Tryouts aren't until Wednesday. We have two gym classes before then. Maybe we'll have soccer again. Maybe Coach Brown will get to see me play."

"That's your only hope," said Lizzy.

2

On the bus ride home from school, Sister told Brother about the tryouts.

"You're going to try out for the team, huh?" said Brother.

"That's right," said Sister.

"I don't know if that's such a good idea, Sis," said Brother.

"Why not?" asked Sister.

"Because you're too small," said Brother. "Coach Brown wants bigger, older girls."

"I can run rings around most of those older girls. I have good moves too. I'm a good kicker. I've scored on *you* lots of times."

It was true. But Brother knew Coach Brown. He knew she liked bigger, older players.

"Well," said Brother, "maybe you should talk to Mama and Papa about it."

"I will," said Sister. "They'll understand."

Mama and Papa did understand. They understood all too well.

"Don't get your hopes up too high, dear," said Mama. "It will be very hard to make the team. The other girls will all be bigger."

"Don't get my hopes up?" said Sister. "How can I make it if I lose hope?"

"Mama just means that Coach Brown wants bigger girls," said Papa. "You shouldn't get upset if you don't make the team."

"I shouldn't get my hopes up! I shouldn't get upset!" said Sister. "*Why* shouldn't I get my hopes up? *Why* shouldn't I get upset? I can run rings around most of the older girls. I'm a better kicker too."

Papa sighed. He could see that Sister wasn't going to listen.

"I'm gonna go out right now and kick Brother's soccer ball around," said Sister. "I have to stay sharp for the tryouts."

Sister left. Mama looked at Papa. "She has her heart set on making that team," she said.

"She's a great little soccer player," said Papa.

"You just said the key word," said Mama. *"Little."*

Papa sighed again. "I know. I just hope Coach Brown gets to see her play before tryouts."

3

Coach Brown didn't get to see Sister play. The next class was basketball. And the next was tumbling.

Soon it was Wednesday afternoon. It was the day of the tryouts. Sister hurried to the locker room. She changed and ran out to the field.

There were forty girls on the field. Some kicked soccer balls back and forth. Some practiced dribbling.

Some just watched. They were *all* bigger than Sister. Much bigger.

Laura Goodbear was there. She was kicking a ball to Bertha Bruin.

Sister ran to Coach Brown. "Reporting for tryouts!" she said.

Coach Brown looked down at Sister. Her eyebrows went up.

"Sister Bear?" said the coach. "What are *you* doing here?"

"I just said what," said Sister. "I'm reporting for soccer tryouts."

"I'm sorry, Sister," said the coach. "I can't allow you to try out. You're much too small."

"Small but good," said Sister. "I can

run like the wind. And I'm tricky. I can stop suddenly. I can twist and twirl. And, boy, can I kick!"

"I'm sorry," the coach said. "You're just too small for the team."

Sister couldn't believe it. Coach Brown wasn't even going to give her a chance!

The other girls had stopped practicing. They were watching Sister and the coach. The coach called, "Back to work! All of you!"

The girls went back to practicing. But they weren't practicing as hard as before. They were still watching.

"We have to start tryouts now,

Sister," said Coach Brown. "I'm afraid you'll have to leave the field."

It wasn't right. It wasn't fair. Coach Brown wouldn't even let her try out. Not only that but she was being kicked off the field! Everyone was watching!

Sister thought she might cry. She didn't want to cry in front of the other girls. She tried to hold back the tears. The harder she tried, the more upset she got.

And that made her cry.

Sister turned and started to walk off the field. She let out a big sigh. It would be a long walk back to the locker room. It felt like the longest walk of her life.

All the girls watched Sister. Coach Brown watched too. She felt sorry for Sister. Suddenly the coach called out, "Wait! Sister!"

Sister ran back.

"Did you change your mind, Coach?" asked Sister. "Are you going to let me try out?"

"No," said Coach Brown. "But I *did* think of a job for you. Team manager."

"What does team manager do?" asked Sister.

"The team manager manages," said Coach Brown. "She does everything that needs to be done for the players and the coach. She's at all the practices and goes on all the team trips. It's a very important job."

Sister thought for a moment. She

didn't really care what the team manager did. She liked the idea of being at all the practices and games. Maybe Coach Brown would see her kick a soccer ball one day.

"Okay," said Sister. "I'll do it."

4

Watching tryouts wasn't a lot of fun for Sister.

She was glad to still be on the field. But she wanted to be one of the cubs trying out.

Then tryouts were over.

After tryouts, Coach Brown told the cubs to look on the board tomorrow. The team would be posted there.

"Who made the team?" Sister asked the coach.

"You'll find out tomorrow," said Coach Brown. "I want all the girls to find out at the same time."

"But I'm team manager," said Sister. "Isn't my first job as manager to know who's on the team?"

"Your first job as manager is to collect the soccer balls," said Coach Brown.

Sister looked around. There were balls out on the field. They were spread all over.

"Okay," said Sister. "Where's the ball cart?"

Coach Brown pointed to a little cub's toy wagon.

"That's not the ball cart," said Sister. "That's a kiddie wagon."

"The ball cart is broken," said Coach Brown. "So I brought my daughter's toy wagon."

Sister looked around again. Cubs were walking home from school. They were walking past the field.

It was bad enough that she hadn't made the team. Now the whole school would see her pulling a kiddie wagon.

"That wagon is too small," said Sister. "It won't hold all the balls."

"Make two trips," said the coach. "Make three trips. Make as many trips as it takes. I'll see you in the locker room."

Two trips? Maybe three? Even *more* cubs would see her pulling a kiddie wagon. *Oh, great,* thought Sister.

She didn't bring the wagon to the balls. She brought the balls to the wagon. It took longer. But she wasn't pulling that dumb wagon.

Finally, it was full. It held only eight balls. She would have to make at least three trips.

Sister waited until none of the cubs were looking. She started pulling the wagon. After a few steps she

started to run. Two balls bounced
out of the wagon.

"Oh, no!" said Sister.

That made the cubs look. They

watched Sister chase the balls and bring them back to the wagon. They pointed and laughed.

Sister started pulling the wagon

again. The cubs laughed even harder. This time Sister didn't run.

It was a long walk to the locker room. The cubs pointed and laughed. Too-Tall Grizzly and his gang of bullies were there. They hooted and hollered like a bunch of monkeys.

When Sister came out for her second trip, there were even more cubs watching. They were all lined up along the fence. It was a nightmare.

It was only her first day as team manager! Could things get any worse?

5

Sister made a third trip with the kiddie wagon.

Too-Tall led the cubs in hooting and hollering. It got even louder this time.

She was glad to get back in the locker room. "Okay, Coach," said Sister. "That's three trips. Twenty-four balls."

"That's fine," said Coach Brown. "But there are twenty-*six* balls in all. You must have left two out on the field."

"Oh, no," said Sister. "I really don't want to go out there with this silly wagon again."

"You don't need the wagon," said the coach. "You can carry two balls in your arms."

"Okay!" said Sister. Maybe not using the kiddie wagon would stop the hooting and hollering.

Was she ever wrong!

"Hey, little girl, where's your wagon?" called Too-Tall.

"Better go get your wagon!" yelled

another bully. "You might drop one of those balls."

The other cubs laughed and laughed. Cubs always laughed when Too-Tall and the gang made fun of somebody—as long as the somebody was somebody *else*. She carried the two balls back inside. She put them in the ball rack. She was glad *that* was over.

"What's next?" she asked.

"Look around the locker room and take a guess," said the coach.

Sister looked around. Dirty towels lay all over the floor and the benches.

"Picking up the dirty towels?" guessed Sister.

"And putting them in that hamper," said Coach Brown.

Sister went around picking up the towels. She dropped them in the hamper.

"Okay, done," she said.

"You forgot one," said the coach.

Coach Brown pointed to the lockers.

There was a towel on top of one of the lockers. It was rolled into a dirty, wet ball.

"Oh, no! Who did that?" asked Sister.

"I think it was Queenie," said Coach Brown. "She did the same thing last year after tryouts. It's her way of breaking in the new manager."

"I'd like to break *her* in," Sister said to herself. She pushed a stool over. She climbed up. She reached for the towel.

The stool wobbled. She almost fell. But she got the towel.

She climbed down and threw it into the hamper. Sister was getting really fed up.

"Is that it?" said Sister.

"That's it for today," said the coach. "You'll do a lot more. You'll carry the water buckets and pass out drinks. You'll go with the team to other schools.

"You'll keep track of the balls, towels, and uniforms," she said. "You'll make sure they're taken on and off the bus with the team."

It sounded like a lot of work. But

it didn't sound like a lot of fun. It sure wasn't getting her any closer to being on the team.

"What's the matter, Sister?" asked the coach. "Don't you like being team manager?"

"You said it was an important job," said Sister. "It doesn't seem important."

"It's very important," said the coach. "Just think, Sister. You take care of balls, towels, uniforms, and drinks. Without those things, we couldn't even *have* a soccer team, could we? Well, could we?"

Sister felt trapped. "I guess not," she said.

"There you go!" said Coach Brown. "So team manager *is* an important job. A very important job. All right, Sister. See you tomorrow at practice."

Coach Brown walked out of the locker room and went to her office.

Sister shook her head. Maybe the job was important. Somehow she just didn't *feel* important.

6

That night Mama and Papa were almost afraid to ask Sister what had happened at tryouts. Brother wasn't.

"Hey, Sis," he said. "What happened at soccer tryouts?"

Sister said, "Coach Brown wouldn't even let me try out. She said I'm too small."

"Well, you *are* too small," said Brother.

"I'm not too small," said Sister. "I'm *good*, and that's all that counts!"

"You *are* good, dear," said Mama.

"Maybe next year," added Papa.

"At least I get to be with the team," said Sister. "I'm team manager."

"Team manager?" said Brother. He rolled his eyes. "*Oh, boy.* Water buckets, dirty towels . . ."

"Stop that," said Mama. She turned to Sister. "It seems like a very important job, dear."

"Well, it isn't," said Sister.

"But *manager*," said Mama. "It sounds so important."

"Sure," said Sister. "Today I got to

manage a bunch of soccer balls and a lot of dirty towels. Tomorrow I get to manage smelly uniforms too."

Brother giggled.

"Want to hear the worst part?" said Sister. "The ball cart was broken. I had to use a toy wagon. The cubs all laughed at me."

Brother laughed. Mama frowned down at Brother.

"Sorry," he said.

But Brother couldn't get the picture out of his mind. He kept seeing Sister pulling that toy wagon full of soccer balls. He started to giggle again.

The giggling turned into laughter. He laughed louder and louder. Tears streamed down his face.

Papa let out a chuckle. He clapped his hand to his mouth. Mama was not amused.

"*You* may be excused, Brother," said Mama. "Go upstairs and do your homework."

"What about dessert?" he asked between giggles.

"When your homework's finished," said Mama. "But before that, tell Sister you're sorry."

"I'm sorry, Sis," said Brother.

But as soon as the words were

out, he started laughing again. He ran out of the room.

"I apologize for your brother," said Mama. "I don't blame you for being mad at him."

But Sister looked sad, not mad.

"I'm not mad at him," she said. "He's right. It must have been a really silly sight. *I* would have laughed at me."

Papa reached over and patted Sister on the back. "That's my girl," he said. "It takes a big girl to admit to looking silly. Don't worry. Things will get better."

Sister thought of something. It made her smile.

"And they *will* get better," she said. "The next time we have soccer during gym class, Coach Brown will see me play. She'll see how good I am. She'll put me on the team. I'm the manager. I know all the players. It'll be great!"

"That's my girl!" said Papa again. "Think positive!"

7

The next day it rained. They didn't play soccer in gym. By afternoon the rain had stopped. The soccer team had their first practice.

The field was wet. It was a sea of green mush and mud.

Before practice Sister passed out the uniforms. They were all fresh and clean. She knew they wouldn't stay clean for long.

After practice Sister collected

the soccer balls. The ball cart was fixed. She was glad.

That didn't stop Too-Tall and the bullies from teasing her.

"Where's your wagon, little girl?" called Too-Tall.

"She must have broken it!" yelled another. Other cubs joined in the teasing too.

As she collected the balls, Sister got angrier and angrier. Was this the way it was going to be all season? Sister wanted to scream.

Finally, she pulled the cart toward the locker room. She wanted to keep her mouth shut. But she just couldn't. When she reached the locker room door, she looked back and yelled, "So long, jerks!"

That only made the cubs laugh and hoot louder.

Sister put the soccer balls away. She looked around. The girls were in the showers.

Their uniforms lay all over the floor and benches. The uniforms weren't fresh and clean anymore. They were covered with mud and grass stains.

"Yuck!" said Sister.

Just then a dirty uniform landed on her head. She yanked it off.

"Double yuck!" she said. She tried to wipe the mud off her face with the back of her hand.

"Sorry," said Queenie. "I thought

you saw it coming."

"Sure you did," said Sister.

A smelly sock hit Sister in the face. And another.

"Pew!" said Sister.

Queenie giggled and ran into the shower.

"Comin' at ya!" yelled another girl.

This time Sister caught the uniform. The socks landed at her feet.

Sister collected the dirty uniforms and smelly socks and put them in the hamper. Then she stood by the showers. She passed out fresh towels as the girls came out.

Sister tried to be nice. "Good practice!" she said to each of them.

The girls snatched the towels out of her hand. No one said "thanks."

Sister went over to Laura. Laura

was drying off. "Hey, Laura," said Sister. "I'm glad you made the team. Good luck."

Laura looked down at Sister. Then she turned away. She started drying her head. Sister couldn't believe it. Did Laura suddenly think she *was* an older girl?

Pretty soon dirty towels started flying at Sister. Sister stuck her arms out to either side. She caught most of them. The rest she picked up and put in the towel hamper.

That was it. Her day's work was done. Thank goodness! Sister headed for the door.

Queenie wasn't done with her yet.

"Hey, water girl!" called Queenie. "Get me a drink!"

Sister glared at Queenie. "Get it yourself," she said.

"But my job is scoring goals," said Queenie. "*Your* job is getting drinks!"

Most of the other girls laughed. Laura Goodbear laughed the loudest. Sister stomped out of the door and headed for home.

8

Sister hoped she would get used to being team manager. At least until Coach Brown put her on the team.

Carrying heavy buckets and getting dirty towels and uniforms thrown at you is kind of hard to get used to.

Coach Brown didn't put her on the team either. The coach never got to see her play in gym class.

After the first week of practice, a

new gym unit started. There were two weeks of tests. It was part of the Bear Country Fitness Program. Lots of sit-ups, push-ups, pull-ups, and running. But no soccer.

Sister never had time to kick soccer balls at practice either. She was too busy managing. Managing balls, water buckets, towels, and uniforms.

Soon it was time for the first game. It would be at another school. That meant Sister would have to make sure all the towels, uniforms, and soccer balls were taken on and off the bus. She would have to work in a strange locker room. She would have to manage on a strange field in front of a crowd of strangers.

At first Sister was a little nervous. But once the players got on the bus, she started to relax.

One reason was the clipboard Coach Brown had given Sister. It had a checklist on it. She got to strut up and down beside the bus and check things off. Then the driver loaded the things onto the bus.

Soccer balls, *check.*

Ball cart, *check.*

Water bucket, *check.*

Uniforms, *check.*

Towels, *check.*

Sister felt the players' eyes on her. That was good. Now she really felt like a *manager.*

She made a few extra check marks just to look more important.

She put her pencil behind her ear and got on the bus. The players were looking at her with respect. Sister puffed out her chest and raised the clipboard. She checked off all the players on her list.

"Everyone's here, Coach," she said. Then she sat down. She got to sit in the front row right next to Coach Brown. *Not bad!* thought Sister.

As the bus pulled out of the parking lot, Sister smiled. For the first time, she felt *important.*

9

The team bus arrived at Beartown School. It was the home of the Beartown Bullies. The Bullies and the Bear Country Cousins were old rivals.

The Cousins filed into the visitors' locker room. Sister passed out the uniforms. Coach Brown led them in a pregame prayer. They ran out to the playing field.

There was a huge crowd in the stands. Sister could tell that the team was nervous. Laura Goodbear didn't just look nervous. She looked *scared.*

Sister wasn't nervous anymore. Managing a real game was different from practice. It made her feel important. And that made her relax.

Sister went up and down the row of players on the bench. She patted them on the back. She said, "You'll do fine."

Sister got some smiles from the players. Laura looked up and said, "Thanks, Sister."

Sister's chest swelled. *This was more like it!* Now she wasn't just managing balls, towels, and uniforms. She was managing the *team.*

But there's an old saying: *Pride goes before a fall.* Sure enough, something happened next that ruined everything.

It all started when Coach Brown said, "The girls look pretty dry. Pass out drinks."

The water bucket! Sister had left it in the locker room. She ran to the locker room. She found the water bucket.

She forgot that there was a hose on the field. So she filled the bucket in the locker room.

Sister walked slowly with the heavy bucket. She walked through the locker room and out toward the field.

The bucket was *very* heavy. It got heavier by the second. Her hand started to hurt. Her arm started to burn.

She wanted to switch hands. But

there wasn't time. She could hear the crowd already. So Sister walked faster.

She hurried toward the field. Her arm felt like it was going to fall off. The bucket was rocking back and forth. The water was sloshing out.

She reached the sidelines. The Bullies were already on the field. The Cousins were standing along the sidelines. They were waiting for their drinks.

Sister started to run. It was like running in deep snow with heavy boots on. Her feet felt like lead. Her hand was going numb.

She reached the sidelines at last. She could hear some of the crowd laughing at her. She had only ten yards to go.

That's when she tripped. She didn't trip over anything on the field. She tripped over her own feet. Sister went head over heels. She let go of the bucket. Water splashed all over. The bucket came bouncing along with her.

It landed upside down *right* on her head! Sister sat there with the bucket on her head. She was dazed.

Someone in the crowd shouted, "Hey, you're in the wrong game!

Helmets are for football!" The crowd roared with laughter.

Sister lifted the bucket off her head. She was soaking wet.

Someone else yelled, "Hey, water girl! The showers are back in the locker room!"

Slowly, Sister picked herself up. She looked out on the field. The Bullies were all laughing. She looked at her own team on the sidelines. *They* were all laughing too!

Laura Goodbear was laughing the loudest. Minutes ago she had been smiling and thanking Sister. Now she was laughing with everyone else.

The whistle blew. The Bear Country Cousins ran onto the field. The Cousins had to start the game with dry mouths.

But did Sister care?
No, she did not.
Sister was mad.

10

For Sister the soccer game was a blur.

She got drinks and towels for the players. But she never even knew the score. (The Bear Country Cousins lost 2–1.)

On the bus ride home she pretended to sleep. The bus pulled into the Bear Country School parking lot. She pretended to wake up.

Later at home, she pretended to eat dinner.

Mama asked, "What's wrong, Sister? Did the team lose?"

Sister stared at her plate. Then she burst into tears. In between sobs, the whole story came out.

Running back to the locker room for the water bucket . . . *struggling* to get the bucket of water to the team . . . *tripping* over her own feet . . . the bucket landing right on her head!

Mama looked at Brother. She was afraid he would laugh. But he looked sad. He had never seen his little sister cry this hard before.

Finally, the sobs stopped. The tears kept flowing quietly. Mama gave Sister a tissue.

Papa cleared his throat. "Well, the main thing is you weren't hurt."

That got Sister to stop crying. She glared at Papa.

"The *main* thing is that I made a fool of myself in front of the whole crowd!" she cried. "If I'd gotten hurt, they might not have laughed so hard. Or called me so many names."

Papa didn't know what to say. He sighed.

"I'll handle this," said Mama. "Come on, Sister. Let's go upstairs."

Mama and Sister went upstairs to Sister's room. They sat together on the bed.

"You know that saying, Mama?" asked Sister. "*Sticks and stones may break my bones, but names can never hurt me?*"

"Yes," said Mama.

"It's not true," said Sister. "Names *can* hurt me."

Mama put her arm around Sister. "I know, dear," she said. "But don't forget, most others aren't really *trying* to hurt you when they call you names. They're just showing off for their friends. I think that's what happened at the soccer game."

"I guess," said Sister. "But getting laughed at hurts too."

"Yes, it does," said Mama.

"I don't want to be team manager anymore," said Sister. "I'm going to quit. The dirty socks and wet towels

were bad enough. But I just can't face the teasing."

"You can quit if you want to," said Mama. "But quitting could just make the teasing worse."

Sister thought about that for a moment.

"I guess so," she said. "Tell you what. I'll go to the next practice. But if anybody says anything about the game, I'm going to make them sorry!"

"You'll do no such thing, dear," said Mama.

"Maybe you're right," said Sister. "They might make *me s*orry. And they're all a lot bigger than I am."

Sister did go to the next practice.

It wasn't much fun. The players did a lot of whispering and giggling. Queenie called her "bucket head" a couple of times.

Laura tried to be like Queenie. Laura called Sister "bucket head" a couple more times.

But Laura had her own problems. She had played poorly in the first game. So Coach Brown kept her out on the field for extra practice.

It made Sister smile for the first time since the Beartown game.

Back in the locker room, she stopped smiling. It was the same old stuff—getting dirty uniforms and dirty towels thrown at her.

After a while Sister was alone in the locker room. Coach Brown and Laura Goodbear were still out on the field. Sister looked around at the messy locker room. It made her sad.

Why did she have to go through this? She wasn't a manager of towels. She was a *player*!

She looked at Queenie's locker. There was a towel balled up on the top again. Something snapped inside Sister. She got angry. *Real angry.*

Sister went over to Queenie's

locker and kicked it. It went CLANG. She kicked a towel on the floor. It went flying over the lockers. She kicked a wastebasket. It bounced off the wall.

She kicked everything in sight until there wasn't anything left to kick.

Then Sister went outside. She kicked a stone so hard it bounced off three trees.

She saw the water bucket. She knew *that bucket.* It was the bucket that had landed on her head at the Beartown game. She hated that bucket.

Sister ran at the bucket. She pulled back her leg and kicked it as hard as she could.

The bucket flew through the air. It landed near Coach Brown and bounced past her.

Sister ducked. Coach Brown was going to yell at her. But the coach didn't yell.

"My goodness!" said Coach Brown. "What a great kick! Come over here, Sister. I'd like you to kick this soccer ball at the goal."

Coach Brown took the soccer ball from Laura and put it at midfield.

Sister ran at the ball. WHACK!

The ball flew straight at the net. It bounced once and went in.

"Wow!" said Coach Brown. "You're the best kicker in the school! You're on the soccer team, Sister! Starting today!"

Sister could hardly believe her ears. She leaped in the air. "Yahoo!" she yelled.

Sister had made the team, after all.

Sister learned something very important that day. Things can go from bad to worse. But they can also get better. Sometimes they can even go from bad to great.

She also learned to be nice to team managers. Not just team managers, but *all* bears with jobs that didn't seem so important. It was a lesson she would never forget.

Sister turned out to be a top member of the team. She even scored the winning goal in her very first game!

And there was one more thing Sister learned that day:

Being small isn't always fun. But it isn't the worst thing in the world either. When you're good at what you do, being small can be *great*.

Check out this excerpt from another
Berenstain Bears early reader chapter book!

The Berenstain Bears'
EPIC DOG SHOW

The Bear family usually did things together Saturday morning. But not *this* Saturday.

Brother and Sister were sitting on the front steps.

Mama hadn't said a word to them since breakfast.

Neither had Papa.

They were much too busy getting ready for the church fair.

Mama was in charge of the bake

sale. She'd been baking cakes and pies all day.

Not that Brother and Sister didn't like cakes and pies.

They *loved* cakes and pies.

But they wouldn't get any of the church-fair goodies. They could just hear Mama if they tried:

"Brother Bear, you get your finger out of that icing! That cake is for the church fair!"

Or:

"Sister Bear, leave that pie alone! It's for the church fair!"

It was the same with Papa.

He was in charge of building things for the church fair. He was building tables for all the sales.

The cubs liked to spend time in Papa's shop. They liked to watch him work. They liked to help. They liked to bring him tools.

But not today.

"Please, cubs," he said. "I don't want to be rude. But the church fair is next Saturday. That's just a week away. I have work to do. I can't have you underfoot."

So they sat on the front steps and felt sorry for themselves.

They could hear the phone ringing inside. But it wasn't ringing for them. It was ringing for Mama.

The sounds of hammering and sawing were coming from Papa's shop. Those sounds were usually music to their ears.

But not today.

Today they just made Brother and Sister feel left out.

The church fair was a big deal in Beartown.

It was held every year.

But it had always been pretty much a grown-up thing.